Based On A True Stori

BASED ON A TRUE STORI

Simernecia Shena

Based On A True Stori

Simernecia Shena

<u>Acknowledgements</u>

My God has been working on me and with me. Saying that I'm blessed is an understatement, my dream was to become an author/writer. I prayed on it and it came to pass, I'm completely focusing on my place in this literary world. I wanted to write a book about life, love, loyalty, greed, sex, and friendships. A wise man once said, "If there is a book you want to read that has not been written, you must write it." Throughout the process of completing my project there were some people who believed in me and my vision. Thank You, for you all have no idea how much this truly means to me. To my daughters, everything I do, my first thought is the two of you, I love you. To my family and friends, whether you've given me advice, motivation, sit downs, laughs, and the tears, I appreciate your presence in my life. Trust me, I know I'm not the easiest person to love, like, and know. You have all inspired me in ways you may never know. Rayshawn Henderson the designer of my book cover, thank you for taking the time to bring my vision to life. To my readers, thank you for letting me into your worlds, minds, and hopefully your hearts.

Viewers Discretion is Advised

Content not suitable for children under 17 years of age.

Based On A True Stori

Based On A

True Stori

<u>The Beginning to the Ending</u>

Earlier today at work, there was an anonymous birthday card mysteriously delivered to me. I wasn't shocked by it, everyone tend to make me feel special on my birthday. Inside of the card there was a small note attached, it said meet me here at 12 a.m., to get your surprise. Me being me, curious to see what the surprise was and who was it from. I followed the directions and the address led me to the local strip club. Strip club?! At the entrance, the young lady checking identification asked my name, handed me a key, and instructed me to head to private room five. I did what she asked, on my way to the room all I seen was, naked women and ass shaking everywhere big asses, little asses, ass, ass, ass all over this club.

I made it to the private hall that was oddly setup like Pandora's box. Smoke all around and women pulling men in every direction. Seriously, I don't know what type of freaky shit is going on, it was not my hype. When I glanced at my watch it was 12:02 a.m., I'm standing directly in front of private room five. I turned the key, and walked in quietly. What my eyes saw next, made everything inside of my body stop. She was riding his dick and he had a tightest grip of her ass.

"Yo pussy is so good." He moaned out.

My heart had just taken all that it could take. The man that I love and dedicated the past four years of my life to, was inside the strip club, fucking a stripper on my birthday. I wasn't interested in stopping them or knowing who she was. This bitch has no idea of the favor she just did for me.

Chapter 1

Stori

<u>What's The Move</u>

I'm not even trying to look at my phone, whatever he's saying is irrelevant. It's 10 p.m. and the text messages are flowing in
back to back. Damn, seriously what does he want? My ex-boyfriend Hakeem has been terrible almost our entire relationship. Hakeem was great in the beginning but, as soon

as he got a little money he changed. I don't know why because I was always good to him. I cooked when he was hungry, had sex when he was horny, paid bills, washed his clothes, and he came home to a clean house. I was honest, faithful, and true. Still that wasn't enough for a motherfucker that wasn't ready. He just wasn't ready, for me and all I had to offer. Not saying I was the best, but bitch you going to learn to appreciate, what you know you're not going to find nowhere else. Hakeem live a lifestyle I could never get used to, he's a jack boy, jealous, a bit controlling and on top of all that, he's a cheater. Hakeem wants to fight every time I catch him down bad.

Based On A True Stori

Now look, I probably was stupid in the beginning but, I got my mind right, quick fast, and in a hurry. Now granted anything I asked for I got, accept for his loyalty and time.

That's what I needed from Hakeem the most. I don't have the time or energy to try and build a man into what I need him to be. We can't continue with these games, it's senseless and pointless. Me and Hakeem decided simultaneously that our relationship was over, Hakeem is having a harder time then I am letting go. That's on him because nothing is going to stop my night out. It's my Birthday! Excuse my manners, I'm Stori Jordan born and raised right here in Baton

Rouge, Louisiana straight from the heart of Sherwood. Today I turned thirty, not trying to brag but, I been the shit. Five foot five, my light brown skin tone kind of resemble a graham cracker, with long black hair that flows down to the middle of my back.

I'm not no skinny chick either, I'm big fine and I carry my weight around well Lb for Lb. My ass and hips are as wide as the Mississippi River, and I'm not mad about it. I just finished getting dressed after trying on two different outfits, I decided on a pure white off the shoulder linen top, with a denim distressed button up mini skirt, paired it with some leopard print Christian

Louboutin red bottoms, and a matching hand clutch. Hakeem gifted me that a few months ago, as a I'm sorry for being a hoe gift. He was excellent at buying, I fucked up gifts. Finished my look off with some diamond earrings, plum lipstick, and my favorite Marc Jacobs Daisy perfume. I was fly and beyond ready to link up with the girls. Before I leave, let me call my girl Jewels to make sure she's ready. Jewels has been my best friend and hairstylist since forever. She's one of those friends that turns into family over time.

I can literally tell her anything and never hear a word of it in the streets. It's the same way with me when it comes to her. To surpass being a great friend, she's one of the baddest hairstylist in Baton Rouge. I Picked up my phone to dial Jewels and Hakeem's messages are the first thing I see.

Hakeem: 9:58 p.m. Stori, I Love you.

Hakeem: 10:02 p.m. I'm not letting go of you

Hakeem: 10:10 p.m. Will you please text me back, damn.

Hakeem: 10:15 p.m. When I say I love you Stori I mean that shit.

Hakeem: Who's gonna love you like me?

" Love! Boy fuck you, that shit dead." I didn't even bother texting him back. How could he think I have anything to say to him, after last night. Hakeem fucked up good this time, ain't no coming back from that. I dialed up Jewels and she answered on the first ring.

"Yes Stori, I'm getting ready now." Jewels said.

"Okay, damn on my way." I ended the call.

When I pulled up at Jewels house, I was expecting her to come straight out. She didn't, so I got out to knock on her door and saw that the bedroom window was ajar. I could hear Jewels inside arguing with her on again off again boyfriend Marcus.

"Marcus I'm going out it's my friend birthday!" Me and Stori are going to have a good time. Why are you trying to stop that? You're always thinking negative about something, dang!" Jewels sounded annoyed.

"You need to be at home." Marcus responded.

"Be here doing what Marcus? You are never even here." Jewels said.

"You right Jewels, just go out." Marcus shouted.

I knocked on the door to end the conversation. She needs to go out, she do not do shit anyway.

"Hold on, I'm coming." Jewels said.

I knocked again

"Dang Stori, I said I was coming." Jewels opened the door with her face beat to the gods.

"Please tell me you're ready to go." I said standing there with a snobbish attitude.

Jewels was hesitant. "Yeah I am."

"You don't sound so sure." I glanced into the house behind her.

"Friend, I'm positive! Can we snap it up before we leave? I need new pictures to post." She said walking out of the door.

Jewels was cute in her white romper and some gold heels that caged around her legs. Her outfit set off perfectly on her mocha skin complexion. Jewels is slim thick, so almost anything is cute on her petite frame. Her hair is beautiful, she has naturally tight curly hair that gives you a fresh out of the shower sexy look my friend was a bad bitch. We are always well put together and when it's time to step, that's what we do, STEP.

"So what's the plans, where are we going?" I asked Jewels as we were climbing into my all black Jeep Wrangler.

"Friend it's your birthday, whatever you want to do. Happy Birthday!" Jewels said while reaching me a card.

"Thank you, Jew! I'm thinking we should try that new club downtown Club 108." I mentioned while adjusting my rearview mirror.

I heard that Club 108 was the new hottest spot in town. On the club's

Facebook page, everybody checks in there. They have a music showcase there tonight for all the local performers. It's supposed to be one artist battling another artist. I guess this should be fun.

"Jewels, can you call Taylor on the aux? I want to make sure she's ready." I asked.

I met Taylor at my job some months ago, I work as a secretary and manager at Excursion Entertainment, we sign all type of clients from music to comedy. Taylor is in the mail/fax room, she delivers mail to all the desk inside the office. Jewels was shady about Taylor. Jewels said something about Taylor rubs her wrong every time she come around. Although

Jewels and Taylor weren't friends, Jewels tolerated her for me.

"Dang Stori, you couldn't tell me your coworker was tagging along before hand?" Jewels was staring me down.

"Listen Best Friend don't be like that, Taylor is not that bad of a person as you think. She really does mean well." I tried to explain.

Sometimes Taylor just don't know how to say things.

"Can you please be nice tonight? Please!" I pleaded, and Jewels picked up my phone as if she rather went back inside.

"What's your password?" Jewels asked picking up my phone.

"Girl please! You been knowing my password for years." I rolled my eyes.

"1206?" She looked back at me. We both bursted out in laughter, and Jewels dialed Taylor.

"Hello." Taylor answered.

"Hey Taylor, what are you doing?" I asked.

"I'm getting ready Stori, about to finish doing my makeup."

"Taylor! You know it takes you every bit of an hour to beat your face." I said knowing she was nowhere near finished. If Taylor drove to the club that'll give Jewels sometime to chill out.

"Well how about you meet us at the club?" I suggested.

15

"Alright that's cool, text me the location." Taylor agreed.

"It's Club 108 downtown." I say and Jewels hung the phone up.

"I don't know Stori but, something about that chick isn't right, and for your sake I hope I'm wrong." Jewels said shaking her head from side to side.

I sighed. "I hope your wrong too."

I've been betrayed a couple times before, so I understand why Jewels felt the way that she did. Once you've crossed me that's it, I'll never speak to you or of you again. The last chick that did some shady shit, was my nail tech Mia. I found out Mia was sending nudes to Hakeem. Even though neither one of

them ever admitted to having sex, I know
they did. I don't put shit past nobody.
Jewels and I caught Mia one day, we beat
the shit out of her. Not over a man but,
how dare she disrespect me like that. I'm
going to die behind my respect no other
way. Taylor doesn't seem as cutthroat as
Mia,
but like I said who can you trust.

   She's mainly a party girl and that's
why I always invite her along.

   "Stori, it's your day and I for sure
don't want to be the reason you don't
enjoy yourself or it's ruined." Jewels was
attempting to put her petty feelings to the
side.

We arrived at the Club 108 and the line was wrapped around the building. We paid extra to skip the line and made our way inside. The inside on Club 108 was crowded. I'm talking jammed tight the only thing left for us, was standing room. Luckily some guys that was trying to catch Jewels and my attention invited us to sit in their VIP section. I hesitated, but the way my feet were set up we gladly accepted. Not long afterwards, we spotted Taylor walking through the doors. I texted her exactly where me and Jewels was sitting at in the club. Taylor walked up in a fitted denim dress it fit her nicely. She was brown chocolate, about five eight, and wore a short pixie cut, it was cute on her. The music was loud and bumping, Jewels was sitting there dancing in her seat, my girl was really enjoying herself and she needed to.

Chapter

2

Danger

<u>Love in this club</u>

It's our official grand opening night at Club 108. We've been operating for about two weeks but, tonight we're expecting our biggest crowd yet. We've connected with local rap artists, to turn tonight into battle rap night. Big Low runs one of the cities hottest studios, he's coming through with his people, to hit the stage and turn the night up. The game plan was to make sure, there was enough staff to make the night run smoothly. My crew was ready to work, 4 barmaids, the DJ, photographer, and my assistant Isaiah.

Being a club owner that was different for me, I've been running the streets majority of my life. Slanging drugs supplying the city. I'm the back bone of my family so I had to find a new way for making money other than dealing drugs. My mother was incarcerated when I was eighteen years old for drug trafficking.

I'm not trying to get jammed up, if I'm in jail and she's in jail then nobody is left to take care of my grandmother. She raised me, she taught me everything I know. I feel forever in debit to take care of her and make sure she's straight, I promise to do that.

My crew is coming upstairs for an important meeting before opening. They all entered and filled my office one by one.

"Listen everyone, tonight is going to be a big night, and a successful night, for all of us at club 108. We have to make sure everything is done in order. If you need anything let me or Isaiah know, and we'll take care of it. Let's have a good night team." I closed the meeting out. Isaiah went down stairs assist with security at the doors. In the matter of minutes, the club was filling up. Everything was operating smoothly as of now, except the bar, as I watched on surveillance video. That's when I saw her, and her friend enter the club. I don't know but, something about shawty grabs my attention every time I see her. I went downstairs to help my bartenders and figured I would give this shit one more with shawty. I'm confident though that if I keep trying, she'll give me a chance.

Chapter 3

Stori

<u>City Nights</u>

There was this guy watching me and Jewels as we entered Club 108 and almost instantly, I remembered him from a brief encounter we had at the Daiquiri Shop on Bluebonnet. Taylor works part time there, and I decided to stop by last Tuesday to finish some paperwork on a new potential artist/client Zek. I was sitting pretty sipping on my usual a green apple martini when he approached me.

"Hello beautiful, is someone sitting here?" He asked.

"Yes, my purse." I shut that down quickly.

"Aww love that hurt, sorry to bother you." He chuckled.

"You're forgiven!" I said looking him up and down, damn he fine. He saw me checking him out too.

"Dang love you are really mean. Continue with whatever it was you was doing. You and your purse have a nice date." He walked off.

Thought he'd never leave.

((FastForward))

25

"Jewels here come Taylor be nice, I'm about to walk to the bar and grab my liquid fix. I know you're not drinking and Taylor probably high as giraffe pussy."

"Hey Stori, Happy Birthday." Taylor greeted me with a hug.

"Thank you, will you ladies please excuse me I'm going to the bar." I was trying to speak over the loud music.

Taylor sat down in the seat where I was sitting next to Jewels and I headed down the steps. Once I reached the bar, I noticed my creepy admirer bartending. He was taking orders however, never came up to take my order. When I glanced away and looked back, that's when I noticed him heading my way with a green apple martini.

"Hello Beautiful, this is your drink, right?" He stood in front of me with a killer smile.

"I haven't ordered yet." I said rubbing my hair back.

"Oh! I know, but I remembered." He smiled.

He can smile at me all day his teeth were so white goodness.

"Oh really? I was almost speechless. Are you a bartender here?" I asked.

"No I'm not, just helping out a little trying to keep the crowd pleased. What brings you here tonight?" He yelled over the loud music.

"Me and my girls are celebrating." I answered.

"Celebrating?" He continued.

Dang his fine ass nosey.

"Oh sorry, it's my birthday." I answered.

My attention was directed dead ass on the stage. I saw Hakeem and his artist Zek, he didn't see me but, why of all places is he here and tonight of all nights.

"Well first off Happy Birthday, I hope you're enjoying your night. I'm Derrick, but everyone calls me Danger and you are?"

"Stori, my name is Stori." I stuttered, his fine ass got me tripping.

"Wow such a beautiful name for a beautiful lady." Danger complimented.

"Are you interested in performing tonight?"
Danger asked.
I'm guessing he noticed my attention, had briefly drifted off.

"Who me? I would never!" Shaking my head.

"A beautiful woman like yourself should be doing so much more on her birthday." He mentioned.

I'm glad that there are still a few men that care. Danger was rubbing his hands together and smiling kind of nervously.

"Are you seeing someone?" Danger asked.

29

Oh Lord, here we go I thought to myself. I'm fresh out of a relationship, what am I supposed to say? Shit I'll just tell the truth.

"No, I'm not." I said cause I'm single now.

"Will I be asking too much, if I asked you to come and take a ride with me?" He half smiled.

"Why would I do that, and a ride where exactly?" I glanced at my phone to see the time it was almost 12:30 a.m., little did he know I was going to go. I just had to see where his head was at first.

"Well, because it's your birthday and around the city. I mean I'm not hard up but, I would love to get to know you

30

more and you get to know me if that's okay with you Love, no pressure." He grinned.

I had a look of admiration in my eyes. He had me right where he wanted me, how can I say no? Not only did he say the correct things but, he looked so good. Danger was about six two, dark skinned, nice medium build, sleepy looking eyes, and those teeth were as white as his sneakers, his grin was so delightful. His gear was fresh too, simple NIKE t-shirt, with matching hoodie, and joggers. He wore a fresh pair of Air Force Ones. His hairline and beard all lined up nicely, he was low key popping. No lies, I was wet the whole time we were talking. Bet the juices from my lady parts could be used as a moisturizer for his beard because, I'm drip, drip, dripping. Am I a hoe if I go? I thought to myself.

"Sure, we can go! Let me tell my girls, I'm leaving and give them my keys. I have to let them know my next move incase you try to keep me." We both laughed.

Jewels texted

Jewels: Stori I see you.

Me: Remember his face. OMW!

"Handle your business love and meet me upstairs in ten minutes." Danger nodded in the direction of another set of stairs.

"Upstairs?" I was puzzled.

"Yes, that's where my office is located. Tell me a four-digit pin number to give security, so they'll let you in." Danger said pointing at some big swole security guards.

"Ummm okay, 1206." I agreed.

As I proceeded to walk off, Danger grabbed me by my arm, pulled me closer, and whispered in my ear, don't keep me waiting." I left.

When I walked off, I could tell he thought I wasn't going to meet him but, I most definitely had other plans. I Went back to tell Jewels and Taylor my next move.

"Sorry to end my night with you lovely ladies but, I'm leaving." Looking back and forward at the two of them.

"Where are you going Stori?" Jewels questioned me with her hand on the side of her face.

"Damn, I'm gonna take a little ride if that's okay with you. See y'all later!" I handed Jewels my keys and Taylor my martini.

"So, you are just gonna leave us like we're not out celebrating your birthday?" Taylor asked.

"Hell yeah! Y'all don't need me, have fun." I took off and headed towards the bathroom first.

When I exited the bathroom, I thought I saw a ghost. Hakeem was standing there waiting on me.

"Happy Birthday Ma how was your d…" Hakeem was holding the bathroom door.

"Thank you, Hakeem! Now if you would excuse me, I have somewhere to be." I said cutting him off.

"I'll see you later tonight right, Stori?" He asked.

"I doubt it, Goodnight." I walked off leaving him standing right where he was.

I went towards the back of the club, before I could make it to the stairs, Danger was already coming down the steps. We left out the club exit and to his car.

"This you?" I was surprised.

"Yeah Luv this me." He chuckled at the look on my face.

We were standing by a all black 2018 Porsche Panamera with tinted windows, that screamed mind your business. Danger disabled his car alarm, opened the door for me, then he went around to the driver's side and got in.

"What's on your mind beautiful?" He asked turning the music down low.

"So, you are kind of flashy I see." I wasn't judging or anything.

"No ma'am not at all. I was just blessed that's it." Danger replied.

"Tell me about yourself." I was curious to know about him.

"Okay, I'm thirty-three years old, don't have any kids, and I'm from here in Baton Rouge. I work hard, I'm a business man, very business savvy you know." He said as he turned onto Main Street.

"And?" I was being nosey.

"I'm single." Danger looked confused.

"And?" I know I was pushing it but, I didn't care.

"I'm the owner of Club 108 and I also own a small restaurant in mid city. Is that enough information for you Ms. Stori?" He said sarcastically.

"Well honestly, I was hoping you would tell me why everyone calls you

37

Danger." I wanted to know if he was involved in any insane activities with a name like Danger.

"Derrick Demond Dangerfield, I've been called Danger my entire life. What you thought, I was a killer are something Stori?" He looked at me and smirked.

"No, I was wondering where Danger came from. I'm guessing Dangerfield Cuisine is your restaurant?" I asked

"Yes, love it is. You like to eat good food? Tell me about you." Danger said.

"Yeah I love to eat. I've been there a few times before the food is bomb! You want to know about me? Well I'm thirty, work with entertainment industries, no kids, hard to deal with easy to love." I answered.

The ride with Danger, was real cool. We pulled up at the levee but, never got out too busy talking. We talked about our recent relationships, I told him about Hakeem and how our relationship wasn't what it should've been. We outgrew one another, and it ended. At least on my end it did. Danger saw me rubbing my arms from the cool breeze, without asking if I was cold, he took off his jacket and wrapped it around me.

"Thank You." I was impressed by how much of a gentleman this guy was.

"You looked cold, back to your last situation, your ex is not over you yet?" Danger squinted his eyes.

"Not quite." I squinted my eyes back.

"That nigga is going to have to let you go." He licked his lips and flashed me that killer smile again.

I could get use to someone like him being around he's different, can't speak to soon though. I'm ready to know about his last relationship, he seems like a good dude. Probably one of those men, that gets tired of you and start cheating just like Hakeem.

"What happened with your last relationship?" My curiosity was at a ten.

"She was involved in a bad car accident, two years ago and died instantly, she was six months pregnant." He cleared his throat.

"I'm sorry to hear that." I could hear the pain in his voice, as he spoke about her. It was silent for a moment.

Danger suggested we go get something to eat, he started his car, and headed down Florida Blvd towards Airline. There was a Waffle House on Airline, he pulled in, and parked.

"What do you know about Waffle House." I said jokingly.

"Say beautiful, I been about that Allstar life." Danger says.

Waffle House had a lot of people per usual. Danger asked me did I mind ordering to go, and I was cool with that. He gave me his order, two all star meals, and a pork chop meal. Although it seemed like a lot I ordered it. We waited fifteen minutes and he went in, grabbed the food and then we left.

"Where are we going?" I asked him while drinking on my orange juice.

"To my house, don't worry I'll have you home before curfew, just sit back and enjoy the ride." He laughed.

We drove to a small gated community in Prairieville, La. Danger's residence, oh my God it was beautiful. His neighborhood was nice and ducked off, he didn't mention if he lived alone and I didn't ask. Danger and I walked into the house through the garage, it was pitch black. There was a little light in the living room, I was amazed at how beautiful it was. I know he didn't decorate all of this by himself. With the WH bag in his right hand, Danger grabbed my hand with his left hand led me up the stairs and to the bedroom. On the way there was a bedroom with a light on, I could see someone walking around inside. When Danger and I entered into what I figured to be his room, he took two of the plates out of the Waffle House bag and walked back out. I sat there at the table waiting on him to return. I looked around,

43

everything inside of his room was pure white and placed perfectly. Then the door swung open and he walked back inside.

"Thought you didn't have any kids." I said reaching for some syrup.

"I don't the food was for my grandmother, she lives with me." He responded.

"Oh sorry." I gotta chill with my sarcasm.

We sat, ate, talked, and enjoyed each other's company. Before we realized it, it was 4 a.m. I was getting sleepy and struggling to keep my eyes opened.

"Well Beautiful, I better get you home." He said.

"Yes, it's getting late, but this was fun." I agreed.

The same way we walked in is how walked out, hand in hand.

Chapter 4

Stori

<u>Wait A Minute</u>

A phone call from Jewels woke me up.

"Hey girl, are you busy?" Jewels sounded disappointed."

"I was just waking up, did y'all have fun?" I asked.

"Yeah, it was okay. Stori what do you know about Taylor's sister Trina? Do you follow her on social media?" Jewels asked.

"Yes, why what's going on?" I was puzzled.

"Stori, Trina is married to Marcus." Jewels started crying.

"Huh! How? When? Jewels I didn't know." I was trying to understand.

"Last night, Taylor said let me call my sister Trina, and tell her, that her husband is in the club. When he should be at home with his pregnant wife. How could he do that to me Stori? After I told him everything I been through, he comes and does some shit like this." I can hear the frustration in Jewels voice.

Jewels has the biggest heart and to hear her in pain was tearing me apart. When she's hurt, I'm hurt.

"Damn Jewels, I had no idea. I follow Trina on Facebook but, she hardly ever post anything. I knew she was pregnant because of Taylor, I didn't know for who though. Honest friend I feel so bad for you, I know how you feel about Marcus." I explained sympathetically.

Jewels have been dating Marcus on and off about two years. They never went anywhere or did anything locally. I told Jewels a long time ago that, that was strange. He would want to take her to New Orleans or Lafayette, I mean why can't he show you off around town, if that's your man? Just fucking me could never be enough but, if she like it, I love it. Jewels had a terrible habit of dating the wrong men, her last ex was abusive and always kept her locked inside the house, literally. While he was around town making babies, with every bitch he put his dick inside of. Truth be told you can't help who you fall in love with, even if the person sells you lies in the beginning and turns out to be a piece of shit. The heart want, what the heart wants, and Jewels heart wanted Marcus.

"I'm so sick of this! I'm sick of going through bad situations, as if I'm not worthy enough for a good man." Jewels was in rage.

"You are girl, don't say that. A man is only going to do what you allow him to do. I promise you that." I cautioned her.

"What am I supposed to do Stori?" She asked.

Truthfully, I didn't know what to tell my girl. I can relate to her because I've been there before, the hurt, pain, and frustration. Yes, it's hard to get over someone you're in love with however, once and when you shake them you shake them. All this information dropped on Jewels at once is a lot to intake. She has to be a big girl and let go of what was. It's going to be times when you feel like you can't go on without someone in your life but, if that person is not for you, they not for you.

"Jewels listen to me, I can tell you to do the most and act an ass or keep it classy and keep it pushing. Nothing is going to come from you acting an ass, that's still his wife and they still have a baby on the way you can't change that. No matter how much he says he loves you, he lied to you." I told her.

"I trust everything you're saying to me Stori and I value your understanding. Marcus needs to give me an explanation and I can't promise you that I won't go upside his head. I'll be by your house in an hour or two to bring your car." We ended the call.

I felt bad for my friend but, we've all had our share of bad men. You have to be strong, let go, and move on.

I dozed off and woke up to Hakeem standing over me.

"So how was your night with your trick ass friends Stori?" Hakeem had an irritable glare.

I knew he would show up sooner or later. That's the types of games he play. I need my key back from him, so I'd better keep this visit pleasant.

"It was great Hakeem. May I have my key back? I don't need you popping up at my house and in my house whenever you want to." I replied.

"I don't have nothing for you. Your girl just pulled off and handed me your car keys here." He stated while handing me my keys.

Why in the hell would Jewels do that dumb ass shit?

"Did you see who was driving her car?" I asked.

"Yeah that Ol nigga she be with." Hakeem responded.

Marcus, I figured that. That's why she gave Hakeem my keys. Jewels didn't want me to see her with Marcus. I don't know what she thought I was going to say hell, that's on her.

"So, this is what you want Stori? You really want to see the monster ass nigga come out of me and why was she dropping your car off anyway, what's up with that?" Hakeem asked.

"Why in the hell are you questioning me? You were just fucking a bitch in the strip club on my birthday. Don't come asking me shit." I spat.

I had to keep pulling the blanket up over me, I didn't want to entice Hakeem in no type of way. Soon as he sees some titties he don't care what we were beefing about he gone smash, even if I say no.

"Hakeem I'm a single woman and can do whatever my heart desire. I don't have to share any of my personal business with you. Why you worried anyway, damn

sure ain't cherish me when you had me."
I explained.

Hakeem wasn't my type but, he was
still very attractive. Hakeem's family is
Indian so that's where his nice skin tone
and good ass hair come from. He keeps
his hair freshly braided going straight to
the back, he was about five ten, and was
so tatted up he didn't have room for
nothing else. Hakeem's body is marked
up like the subway in Harlem. I can't
even lie the kid is raw and he can dress
his ass off but, that attitude makes him
ugly plus his dick was bullshit. Yeah, I
know that's mean but, it's the truth. On
an easier note he can eat pussy like a
champion. I'm not going to miss the head

though, Hakeem is a damn nag and I'm tired of him.

"I'm gone Stori." He walked off.

I'm going to remember to make a note to get my locks changed, I know he made a copy of my key that's the kind of shit he does. Whenever Hakeem comes around, I make sure to keep our conversation at a bare minimum, he has a problem with his hands and I'm the bitch that fight back period.

Chapter

5

Stori

<u>Family Ties</u>

I've been seeing Danger steady about three weeks now. Everything is elevating just how it's supposed to be. We talk every day and probably have seen each other a handful of times since the night of my birthday. I like Danger more so because he's never not even once mentioned sex. He was able to capture my attention without even touching me. That's one hundred, a text came through and it was him

Danger: Hello Beautiful, how are you?

Me: Hey, I'm great hru?

Danger: I would be great too, if I could see you.

Me: Okay.

Danger: Can you meet me at the Chase Bank on Government?

Me: Yes, I'll meet you there.

I put my phone down and got in the shower. That hot shower did everything to my body. I stepped out, dried off, and rubbed down with my Bath and Body

Works Beautiful Day. Threw on my V.S PINK leggings, with matching tee, wrapped my pullover around my waist, slipped on my UGGS, brushed my hair, grabbed my wallet and shot of the door. When I made it to bank, I spotted Danger's car parked.

Danger: My door is unlocked.

Hopped out of my Jeep and went to his car. When I opened the door, a bouquet of red roses sat on the passenger seat with a note attached it said "One Day".

Me: One Day what?

Danger: One Day you'll be mine.

I smiled grabbed my roses and placed them on the backseat but, not without realizing there were some daisies back there. What the hell he got going on? I thought to myself. I read the note on them too, I Love you Granny.

Danger: Stori you nosey lol.

Me: So

He made his way out of the bank and came to the car.

"Thank you for the flowers, they're beautiful." I greeted.

"You're welcome, I'm glad you like them." Danger kissed my hand.

"What was taking so long." I asked.

"The bank teller had a hard time resetting my safes at Club 108 and home." Looking into his phone.

I sat there and enjoyed our lil ride. We went to get his grandmother something to eat, and took it to her, along with her flowers. The way Danger drove, with one hand on my thigh and the other one on the steering wheel, it was so sexy to me. I've learned so much about him and his background. He came from a long line of drug dealers it started with his granny. When Danger got in the game at fourteen years old, he learned the ways of the streets from his grandmother, she used to take him with her to catch her plays. When he was ready, she connected him with all her plugs and everything else was set in stone for him.

"I'm not physically out in the streets anymore, I've lived on the wrong side of the law long enough to know how it works. I'll be done with this life soon enough. My grandmother needs me to care for her." His face was solemn.

It was good to hear that he never touches the product, just pick up the profit. The hard part for me to believe is that he can just up and leave the game. Once you get accustomed to making fast money it's hard to let go of. Danger went on to say that his granny was recently diagnosed with Amyotrophic Lateral Sclerosis (ALS) and he knows he has to be there for her. I met his granny a few weeks ago and wouldn't have known that little sweet lady was a queen pin of her era. Grams was the shit!

Based On A True Stori

Sitting inside of Danger's office at Club 108 watching him handle his business, he was so sexy while he was working. The office was pieced together perfectly too. His desk sat by a large tinted window, the kind that no one can see in but, you can see out. I was sitting on a nice red sectional sofa in the corner, every time Danger took a phone call, he stared at me. He does not have to watch me, I'm not going nowhere I thought to myself. Danger and I were starting to be intrigued with each other, I wanted to be everywhere he was. The fact that he could show me so much attention and how much he cared in such a short period of time meant a lot to me. I wish he

would've come into my life years ago,
then I probably wouldn't be such an
emotional wreck or so guarded. The DJ
inside the club was banging, he was
playing Tank's fucking with me. That's
my shit! Danger motioned for me to
come over to his desk. I walked over
while he was in the middle of a business
phone call.

He smiled, grabbed me by the waist,
and pulled me down onto his lap. I could
feel his manhood rise immediately,
Danger looked at me and grinned.

"Yeah that's a bet, double this pack
for me and it should seal the deal for a
few months." He ended the call.

Based On A True Stori

I wondered what type of codes he was talking in, to whoever was on the line. Whoever it was he wasn't focused on the conversation any more, his attention was on me. The harder his dick got the wetter my cat was. Danger stood up with me still attached to him and walked over to the sofa where I was originally sitting. The way that he was protectively holding me did something to my soul. He reached over turned off the lights, and locked the door. All I could think of was, I don't know what's about to happen but, it better be good. When Danger kissed me, he was so passionate, when he touches me it sends chills trough my body.

Before I knew it, he was kissing all over me. He was licking my legs, then he started kissing on my kitty, his lips and tongue felt so amazing. Danger didn't miss not one single spot.

"I want to feel you inside of me." I moaned.

He flipped me over and without pressure, he plugged his dick inside of me. My body needed and wanted this so badly. Not just the sex but, the physical attachment from somebody that cared. Danger was constantly kissing my forehead, sucking my titties, rubbing my hair, and stroking me at the same time.

"Oh baby, what are you doing to me?" I screamed.

"I want you to fall in love with me Stori." He growled.

I was holding onto the pillow, off of the sofa, as my pleasures begin to erupt one after another. Danger exploded inside of me and collapsed softly on top of me. We cradled up closely and fell asleep. Damn I was in my feelings but, in a good way. We laid there underneath each other until Club 108 closed. At closing Danger and his employees shut the club down. He locked up and drove me to the bank to retrieve my Jeep, then followed me home. When I arrived at home all I wanted to do was shower, plug in my earbuds, turn Ella Mai Naked on repeat, and dream about the night I had just experienced with Danger. That's exactly what I did.

Chapter 6

Jewels

<u>This Is It</u>

Marcus you are a lying manipulating bitch! I was practicing my argument for when Marcus walked through the door. This man had taken advantage of me, he had the ability to ruin my reputation with the lies he's told. Like a fool in love, I believed every word he's ever said to me.

A wife and a baby, I said the words out loud but, couldn't believe what was coming out of my mouth. I was standing at the opening of my laundry room when I heard the kitchen door open. My heart wanted me to stay calm but, I couldn't. I screamed and went after him but, he held my hands above my head in the air.

"You are a liar! You required me to be submissive to you and you have a wife, a wife that's pregnant!" I screamed and cried.

He stood in front of me and didn't say anything just looked at me with complete guilt in his eyes.

"How dare you! How fucking dare you Marcus?" I sobbed.

"I'm sorry Jewels." He spoke.

I've wasted away two years of my life in love with someone else's husband. All because he couldn't be honest.

"You're sorry! You're sorry!" I yelled with tear filled eyes.

How is sorry supposed to heal me from the damage he's caused my heart?

"I was a wonderful woman to you, I catered to you, and I shouldn't have, it wasn't my responsibility. It was your wife responsibility!" I reminded him.

There were nights where Marcus came to my house and mistreated me, took this anger out on me. I still tried to make it work because I thought he loved me.

"Listen to me!" He raised his voice.

"First of all, don't raise your voice at me." I said still with my hands in the air.

"I'm sorry Jewels, what more can I say?" He dropped my hands.

I can finally hear the regret in his voice, he sounds sorry. He looked at me like he knows what I'm going to say next.

"Marcus get out, leave now!" I say with my back towards him.

"This is it, right Jewels? He asked.

I didn't even have to think about my answer.

"You damn right!" I said through my tears.

Chapter 7

Stori

<u>Back to Business</u>

My alarm clock goes off at 7:30 a.m. scaring the hell out of me. After pressing random buttons to kill the sound, it finally stops. I laid back down to prepare myself for the day ahead. I have an important meeting today, if I close the deal it'll be my chance to step up the ladder at Excursion Entertainment. That's what I really want, it means more pay and more benefits. After finally getting out of the bed, I decided to put on a black button up silk shirt of course I left it open a little, a black tight fitted knee length skirt, I paired it with a thin orange belt and some orange YSL sling backs. My hair was done in a roller set by Jewels a few days ago and it was flawless. I checked my watch it was almost 8:15 a.m. if I hurry, I'll make it to my meeting on time.

Three hours later I'm sitting in my office looking over contracts for my new client, Zek. The meeting was a success, as I knew it would be. Although I don't want to deal with Hakeem at all, Zek is good for business. Danger hasn't called but, I know he will. Now that I think of it no one has called me all day. Not, Danger Jewels, not even Hakeem. It's odd, because normally my phone lines are blowing up. Someone knocked on my office door.

"Yes, come in." I answered.

"Hey girl! What you been up to?" Taylor asked closing the door behind herself.

"Nothing much." I responded.

Taylor look at me side eyed. "You sure Stori? Because from the looks of it you've been up to a lot." Taylor said standing with her hand on her hips.

I didn't know what Taylor was talking about or where she's going with this conversation. Taylor is cool but, I don't tell her much of my business. For one she works with me and two we weren't not friends like that.

"I heard through the wind you closed the deal on Zek." She finally said.

"Yep." I nodded.

"That's not all though?" Taylor was reaching for her phone.

"Spill it bitch!" I rolled my eyes.

Taylor pulled out her phone and showed me screenshots of Danger and I together. The pictures are from different nights in the club. It's not hard for one person to put two and two together. I did notice a photographer in Club 108 but, I didn't pay any attention to the thought of him possibly posting pictures on social media. There was a picture of us standing by the bar and pictures of him following me upstairs.

"What's good Stori, are you entertaining Danger?" Taylor continued.

"He's cool." I said quietly.

She knew I wasn't going to say shit, so she let it rest.

"I have something else to tell you." Taylor said.

Lord they have a video of me and Danger fucking or something.

"I'm listening." I had a straight face but, my heart was beating like a drum.

"So also on the Facebook page was my sister husband Marcus talking to Jewels. I mean I know that's your friend and Trina is very bold when it comes to her husband." Taylor stated.

What I am not about to do is discuss Jewels business with Taylor. I don't care how stupid I think Jewels is about Marcus, that's not a conversation for me and Taylor.

"Taylor, Jewels is a grown woman if you or anyone else have anything to ask her, ask her. Better yet if you feel like she's involved with Marcus ask him. The only person that owes your sister marriage something, is her husband." I said.

Taylor should've known better and I'm ready for her to leave, so I could call Danger about these pictures.

"Damn Stori, I'm sorry!" Taylor apologized.

Taylor didn't mean any harm but, I had to let her know.

"It's okay." I reached for my cup.

"Stori, we have Karaoke tonight at the Daiquiri Shop, you should come by." Taylor extended an invite.

"Okay! I'll let you know but, you'll have to excuse me I have a very important call to make." I ended our conversation.

Taylor left my office and the first person I needed to call was Jewels. I FaceTimed Jewels.

"What are you doing, you have a minute?" I asked.

"About to do my last client. What's up? You never call me while you're at work." Jewels had a confused look on her face.

"I've been told that there's a pic."

"Picture of me and Marcus on Facebook arguing, yeah I know. Marcus wife asked him about it and he asked me." Jewels cut me off.

"Oooooh." I squinted.

"Not that I give a damn about a picture being posted, I mean after all this

80

time I finally know why he wouldn't allow me to post us." Jewels said.

"Do you want to go out for drinks?" I asked.

"Yes Stori, that would be great. My client is here so I'll call you back." She replied.

I opted not to call Danger about the pictures. He's single and so am I what's understood don't need to be explained.. My work day is complete and I'm ready to go home, get out of these clothes, walk around naked and relax.

After I made it home and couldn't sleep, I decided to clean around the house and meet up with Jewels for drinks. I arrived at the Daiquiri Shop before Jewels, and thankfully I did because guess who's sitting there, Trina. Now I'm aware Taylor invited me and not Jewels. Taylor also knows me and my girl go out together. I texted Jewels to see what she wanted to do.

Me: I'm at the Daiquiri Shop and Trina is here.

Jewels: Okay, I'm already outside and promise to keep it classy.

Me: Are you sure?

Jewels: Walking inside.

I was sitting there looking pretty in my royal blue bodycon from F21, a multicolored flora scarf wrapped around my hair, some pink closed toe heels that matched my scarf perfectly, and a bomb ass GUESS bag, simple but, cute. Jewels walked through the door, looking like a bitch that's fresh out of a bad relationship and ready to do damage. She wore some white denim pants that were so distressed they didn't have much material left, a nude lace bralette that showed off her nipple piercings, some double strap nude sling backs, and her hair was on point as usual.

"Okay Friend, I see you!" I gassed her up.

"Thank you Stori, you know I try but, not that hard." Jewels laughed.

We ordered our drinks and watched the Karaoke performers hit the mic one after another. Jewels was facing me, so she didn't see how much Trina kept eyeing our table. She looked so much I wanted to ask her, what the hell she was looking at. When I noticed Trina was walking to the stage to perform. Taylor texted.

Taylor: If Trina does something stupid, I have nothing to do with that. I didn't know Jewels was coming.

The host had the microphone.

"Let's welcome—" Trina grab his microphone.

"Let's welcome this home wrecking bitch Jewels to the stage. Stalking me on social media, sleeping with married men, and breaking up happy homes." Trina announced

I know she didn't! The look on Jewels face was so calm. Trina begin walking towards us in the audience.

"Taylor get your sister!" I yelled.

"First of all, Ma'am you can't break up a home that you never knew about from the beginning. I don't owe you nor your marriage a bitch ass thing pussy ass hoe!" Jewels shouted.

Now Trina and Jewels are face to face.

"Oh yes Bitch, you owe me! You're walking around here wearing the smiles that my husband should be giving me!" Trina screamed.

Trina was shaking, crying, and pointing her finger in Jewels face. That was the biggest mistake she made, and

she was about to soon find out why.
Before I could pull Jewels out of the way
it was too late. Jewels had already tased
Trina.

"Jewels she's pregnant!" I screamed.

"Fuck that bitch and her baby! She
don't have no business being out here
pregnant and starting trouble. Probably
why her husband cheated on her!" Jewels
spat.

I heard Taylor saying something, I
don't know what and I don't care because
I told her to get her sister.

Chapter 8

Taylor

Bang for Bucks

The phone ring disturbed my concentration.

"What's up Trina." I answered my sister call.

"Taylor, that bitch Jewels is gonna pay for her fucking sins. All the men in the world, and she chose to suck on my husband dick." Trina said.

"Trina, I'm not about to get involved in that mix. I have enough shit going on." I replied back.

Ever since we were little, I have been falling behind my sister but, I be damn if I chest up for her behind her trifling ass husband Marcus. Marcus wasn't shit when Trina married his ass and Trina knows that.

"I didn't ask you to get involved Taylor, I know how to handle this." Trina added.

I wasn't trying to be rude or make my sister feel like I don't have her back. I'll always have her back, just not when it comes to bullshit ass Marcus.

"I'm glad you know sister, I'm out here chasing these coins baby girl. Trina, I didn't want to tell you this but, I have been working at the strip club part time." I told my sister

"Oh Taylor, that's on your body, you grown! Trina announced.

Yeah, I picked up a part time job as a stripper. Struggling to make ends meet and paying for college was getting the best of me. In my opinion, a bitch better do what she has to do to make it. Mentally no I didn't want to dance but, financially I didn't have many other options. I collect more money stripping, then I make at the Daiquiri Shop and inside of the mail room at Excursion Entertainment. It's different from the ruthless shit I used to do. I had to change my ways, because where I'm from that shit will get a bitch knocked off quickly.

Chapter 9

Stori

<u>Late Night Creep</u>

Tonight, was a night, thinking I would come home to peace, it only got worse.

"Where have you been Stori?" Hakeem spoke in the dark.

"Hakeem, why are you here?" I was livid.

I knew he would make a duplicate of

my house key, I should've changed my damn locks. It didn't matter though, Hakeem is the type of nigga that would kick in my door to get his point across.

"Who is this new nigga, I'm hearing about you being all around town with?" Hakeem asked.

He probably didn't hear shit, probably saw it on Facebook like Taylor did. Hakeem should've known it would come to this. If you don't cherish what you got, another man is gonna take your spot.

"Why? You don't have anything to do with what I have going on. What you need to worry is all of, these little bucket headed hoes, you dealing with and slinging dick to like Baton Rouge not number one for HIV!" I responded.

"Stori I'm not trying to hear all that, end the shit before things get ugly Ma! I told you the only way out of this relationship is death." He was angry and so was I.

I could literally argue with Hakeem all night but, tonight is not the night.

"Hakeem will you please leave, I'm tired. I've had a long night and day." I tried to end our conversation.

"Go to sleep then! You had a long night entertaining that nigga! I'm staying here tonight. Stori you're not about to have another nigga in here Ma, and you're definitely not about to live happily ever after with no other man. So, put an end to it before I do it, because then shit is going to turn out bad!" Hakeem walked off.

Now how in the hell did I get myself into this situation? Plus, Danger is a little fucked up too. I don't need nothing bad to happen and that's the part that frightens me.

I drifted off and woke up to Hakeem tapping me on my shoulder.

"Stori, your phone is ringing." He said holding my phone.

"Put my phone down! I'll call them back." I was aggravated.

My phone started ringing again.

"Hello."

You have a collect call from:
Jewels…at the East Baton Rouge Parish
Prison.

"Now what the hell she done did?" I said
out loud.

To accept these charges, dial 1.

"Jewels?" I answered.

I put on my robe, grabbed my purse,
and walked outside.

"Stori, I'm in the parish. That bitch
Trina went to the cops and pressed
assault charges against me, with the
daiquiri shop incident. She didn't know
where I lived but, everybody in Baton
Rouge know I do hair, so they came to
the salon and arrested me." She
explained.

"How much is your bond?" I asked pulling out my checkbook.

"Don't worry about that, I'm waiting to be released. Marcus paid my bail, that's on that retarded bitch, taking money out of her own household. Anyway, that's not what I called for, I called about your little friend Taylor. Now didn't I tell you that girl wasn't your friend, a lil chick in here say she knows Taylor and Trina and neither of them are to be trusted. The chick said Taylor is a setup bitch. I don't know though." Jewels said speaking with no hesitation.

"Well Jewels, that don't have nothing to do with me. Taylor never did shit to cross me, I spoke with her about the situation with you and Trina. She already knows not to get involved because I'll have to get involved. It's not a matter in taking sides that's her sister and you are my friend. If the shits pop off, I'm riding for you, that's law!" I told Jewels.

"I feel that! Still don't trust that bitch though and another thing you know she fucking with Zek, so if Hakeem finds out your business that's why." Jewels stated.

"Uh-huh, well yeah I'll have to limit information I share with her, even though I don't tell her nothing about me and Danger. So that's the least of my worries. Back to you, you back fucking with Marcus?" I responded.

"No, I just needed him to bond me out, I'm done with him." She explained.

I knew she was lying but, she's gonna have to learn on her own.

You have one minute remaining the operator cut in.

"Uh Huh Whatever. I love you girl." I added.

"I love you too." Thank you for using Evercom.

After I hung up with Jewels, I couldn't stop thinking about the past few days, and how I've been ignoring Danger. He didn't deserve the silent treatment from me. He's been calling and texting but, other than the simple I'm okay hru text, I haven't been responding. The only reason I did send that was because I didn't want him to think something was wrong and pop up.

Then he'll see Hakeem here, I feel like I owe him an explanation as to what's going on but, he wouldn't understand. Now that's my truths. I don't want to be with Hakeem, no we're not fucking, or none of that, he's just at my house blocking.

Chapter 10

Taylor

<u>Blood Thicker</u>

All this drama between my sister and Jewels was pure entertainment to me. The reality behind it is, Trina was not going to let it rest. She never lets anything go, that's why I told Stori to warn Jewels because the shit could get bad. Stori also need to know what position I play and of course that's backing my sister. Our parents weren't shit, but they taught us that much. Even though I tell Trina I have nothing to do with her

Shenanigans we all know what's up, if it pops off. Stori's home girl Jewels don't like me and I don't care. I'll still go around to get information, the both of them know what's up around this city and I'm going to level up by any means. Even if it's at the cost of another bitch. It's like doing something you don't want to do but, you do it anyway. Somebodies got to get it and it ain't gonna be me.

I'm getting ready for to work my night at the strip club and I just remembered, one of the guys owe me some money. He's one of the high spenders, always popping off good money. The last time the dude asked for a private dance, he claims he only had a card so he couldn't pay. He did say he'll pay more the next time. Today is the next time

and I will have my cash app available,
incase ol boy want to play games.

Chapter 11

Stori

That's What Friends Are For

The sunlight was beaming through the window, it nearly blinded me. I laid in my bed pondering what my next move was going to be. I thought on taking a break with Danger. Not because I don't like him, I like him a lot, too much actually. Still having Hakeem popping up is a deal breaker, I don't want to hurt

Danger he's a good man and he's good to me. It's just risky having them both around cause clearly, Hakeem will not go ahead about his business. The hardest part is letting Danger know. I wanted to call him but decided to text instead. I got out of bed and went to the bathroom.

Me: Hey

Danger: Hey Beautiful

Me: Are you busy? I wanted to talk to you about something.

Danger: What's on your mind?

Me: I think our relationship is progressing quickly and we need a little break.

Danger: So that's what you do Stori get me wrapped up into you and leave?

Me: Actually! It's my Ex he's putting me in a complicated situation.

Danger: You think imma let you go cuz of some bitch ass nigga lol nah Love it's not that easy.

Me: I don't want issues.

Danger: That's dead, I'll see you tonight.

That didn't go as planned. Hakeem is swearing on how much he's changed but, it's much too late he should've changed when I needed him to change. All the shit I've been through with Hakeem and the things I've accepted from him, I knew better.

I got up and dressed and left out to start my day. A lunch date with Jewels is just what the both of us needed. After she touched up my hair at the salon, we decided to go eat at Tokyo Grill. While we waited to be seated Jewels was receiving a ton of messenger video calls.

"Stori, I don't know who keeps calling me every time I try and answer my call drops. Jewels said trying to get her phone to work.

"Turn on the WiFi." I said.

I've been stuck in the house or at the office, so this little spa lunch date was right up my alley. I've been ignoring Danger still and I know he's feeling some type of way by the text he's been sending. Today he texted.

Danger: If I don't see you tonight, I'm pulling up at your job and your house.

105

I didn't even reply to his message and my gut was telling me that he wasn't playing.

"Jewels, I have to tell Hakeem I'm done. I miss Danger so much." I whined while looking through the menu.

"You sure do! We all know people stick around, when they know you have the ability to move on and find better. That's just what Hakeem is doing." Jewels sipped her drink.

Jewels paused and was looking in her phone at her phone with a foul look on her face.

"What's wrong Jew?" I asked.

She was silent.

"Jewels!" I spat.

"Someone sent me a picture of Marcus in the bed." Still fidgeting with her phone.

"Trina?" I asked cause she's in to playing pill head games.

"No Stori, not Trina." Jewels had a vacant expression.

I was anxious. "Well who?"

When Jewels turned her phone around and showed me her screen.

"Oh my God! I know you are lying!! Is that a transgender?" I was shocked.

Jewels didn't say one word, but the look on her face said everything. I knew he wasn't right! How you fuck your wife and two side pieces, one of which is a male. That's another level of trifling. If you want to be gay be gay, but don't be a down low nigga trying to do the shit in the dark. He around here putting everybody life in jeopardy trying to live an undercover life. People would respect you more if you were real about your sexuality. And plus, he acts like the transgender community don't expose secrets just like everybody else does.

"Jewels, you don't have to say anything just listen. Save yourself the embarrassment, public humiliation, and leave his life silently. It's not like, the world knew about you being with him. Ain't one man in this world worth all the shit Marcus has put you through. Let

Trina keep her husband, he is her problem not yours." I explained.

I sat there and watched those tears flow down my friend face.

"Stori, I feel like needles are poking me in my eyes." Jewels cried.

"I said what I had to say and I'm not taking it back. It gets better trust me." I say.

Chapter 12

Stori

<u>I Want, What I Want</u>

Today I'm going to tell Hakeem it's over. I made myself remember all the shit, I tried to forget. All the hurtful things he's ever done, and I've come to the conclusion that today is the day. Now this can go one or two ways, he'll flash out and try to fight, or he'll just leave.

I'm scared to death but, it's time. Hakeem walked into the living where I was.

"Hey, we have to talk about something. It's too late to rebuild our broken relationship. Hakeem I can't take you back and I don't want you back, I'm in love with someone else." I explained.

"Danger? Stori what I saw on Facebook is true? What people are saying around town is true Stori?" Tears slowly rolling down his face.

"Yes Hakeem, things between us developed he's good for me. We've been seeing each other for a while. I want to start a life with him Hakeem, I love him." I said.

"Really Stori? You think I'm going to let you be happy with another man? I will make your life a living hell!" He's standing there with a horrible snarl on his face, like someone forgot to take out the trash.

That did it. Hakeem has brought nothing but, turmoil into my life, when he should've been my peace.

"And at this point, you have no fucking choice! You think I'm going to keep letting you fuck random bitches on me? And then you'll fuck around and give me something I can't get rid of! Fuck no! Get your shit and get the fuck out of my house!" I screamed and walked out of my front door.

I left for a few hours and when I came back home it was dark outside. Hakeem had left and took all of his things. The only thing on my mind, was to see Danger. I texted him to come over and waited patiently for him to show up.

Glaring out the window waiting on Danger to arrive, I needed him to pull up so we could talk. I had to prove to him that he was what I wanted and needed, he's my baby. My phone went off.

Danger: I'm outside.

Me: Okay, I'm coming.

I went outside to his car, when I got in everything was silent at first. I just threw my hands on my face and held my head down.

"What's up Stori?" He asked.

"I'm sorry, I miss you. Danger I was wrong, and I shouldn't have avoided you the way that I did." I whined, and his phone started ringing.

"Hold up Love, I have to take this call." He showed me his phone.

"Yo, yeah my boy I'll have everything next week." Danger said.

He was sitting in that driver seat looking like a snack. Temptation was rushing me and my hormones were raging. I leaned in and started kissing him, licking all over his ear. He was still holding the phone whoever was on the other end was talking to him and he was listening carefully. I unzipped his pants exposing all of him. With no hesitation I inserted all his manhood, deep inside of my warm mouth. I wet it good and was slurping him up, like he was a piece of world's finest chocolate.

"Aye I'm kind of in the middle of something. I'll call you back with the numbers." He hung up.

I crawled in the backseat, pulled off my panties, and slide them under the seat. In case he thought about having another woman in here, she'll know I was here first. Danger got out and joined me in the backseat. He returned the favor, it was so good I moaned with every lick he laid on me.

"Shit baby, I want you." I moaned in full pleasure.

He's always gentle and nasty too. We decided to finish inside, never made it to my bedroom.

"Stori, do you trust me? He asked.

"Yes, baby I do." I answered him.

Placing sweet kisses on my inner thigh. I hope he knows what he's doing, my cat is too tight for him to insert all that dick at once. We engaged in more foreplay, he blew on my pussy and gently twisted my breast nipple between his wet fingers that he pulled out of my special place.

When Danger got on top of me to insert his joy stick into my pleasure hole, he took his time and eased it in inch by inch.

"Ooooowee." I moaned.

"Am I hurting you? He stopped.

"No, go harder." Shit I wanted to be a big girl, I wanted that dick.

Thankfully, I don't have any neighbors because he made love to me like he was punishing me.

Chapter 13

Jewels

<u>Repairing Me</u>

Stori arranged for me to take domestic violence sessions. She knew I wouldn't have set up the sessions myself, so she scheduled them. Today was my first meeting. Stori explained to me how important she thought it was, for me to speak with someone, about the mental and physical abuse I've experienced. I

118

agreed with her, I need to grow from the pain I was affected by. As I looked for a parking space around the building, I looked at how it was an old and outdated establishment. I thought twice about going but, went inside anyway. The counselor was standing there, greeting everyone that came in.

"Hello everyone, I'm Mrs.Thomas. Please have a sit." She said.

She instructed the group that we'll go around the circle to introduce ourselves, and what we are a victim of. We got started quickly.

"Hey everybody, my name is Phoenix."

"Hey Phoenix." We all said in unison.

"I'm a victim of molestation as a child." Phoenix said.

"Okay Phoenix, what do you plan on taking away from this group?" The counselor asked.

"My hope is to be able to trust people again. I want to stop thinking everyone is out to hurt me because of my past." Phoenix says.

"That's what we are here for, to help you press forward." Mrs. Thomas said.

Mrs. Thomas signaled to me, letting me know that I was next. I swear I didn't know what to say. I wanted to forget all the things that caused me pain.

"Hello, I'm Jewels, I'm here because of my history of being involved in

120

domestic and verbal abusive relationships. My plan is to leave this group a stronger me. I want my strength back from where it was stolen from me. I allowed the people I thought loved me, to misuse me." I spoke and was proud that I was finally, opening up.

Mrs. Thomas stated that it would be easier to work with us in groups of two. She paired me and Phoenix together. Our assignment was to try and understand the others situation. Figure out how to help each other grow. The meeting ended, we exchanged contact info with our partners, then was dismissed. Over the next course of days Phoenix and I met up. Phoenix told me about being molested by a family member as a child. I spoke on the things that hurt me, mostly what I went through with Marcus. Stori was right I needed this, I needed to be able to talk to someone to heal. How did I let myself get to this point I don't know but, I'm definitely on my road to recovery.

Chapter 14

Stori

<u>IKYFL</u>

Me and Danger switched cars today. My car needed to be serviced, and I had a doctor's appointment for my yearly female exam. He agreed to take my car to get checked and joked about me wanting to ride fly in his car. I made it to the doctor's office and signed in, I was already running late. In the waiting area

Trina was there, this bitch better not start no shit, I thought. The man she was with was not Marcus either, and they were well acquainted too. He was rubbing her belly and all. Well damn! That's Big Low he's always with Hakeem and Zek, it's a small world.

"Jordan?" The nurse called.

"Yes." I walked to the door where she was standing.

"Ms. Jordan can you please urine in this cup please and meet me in room two? The bathroom is down the hall to your left." She told told me.

I walked out of the bathroom holding my pee cup, Trina was there. Here we go again.

"Listen Stori, tell your friend Jewels to leave my husband alone, if she doesn't want any problems." Trina said.

"First of all, my friend, do not want your gay ass husband. You need to worry about the punk that's putting pictures of Marcus all on social media and not Jewels! Now bye." I replied and walked to room two. The fuck she thought.

I sat in the exam room and waited for the doctor to come in. Twenty minutes later she came in holding my chart.

"Hello Ms. Jordan, How are you? Dr Patterson greeted.

"I'm fine." I said.

"Are you on any medicines?" Dr. Patterson asked.

"No, I'm not." I answered.

"Well, I'm going to start you on an iron pill and a prenatal vitamin.

"Prenatal?" I was confused.

"Yes prenatal. Congratulations Ms. Jordan, you're expecting." Dr. Patterson stated.

I was confused and happy at the same time. My own little baby is growing inside of me. When I left the doctor's office, I was eager to share this with someone. I stopped, got pizza, and went by Jewels house. Jewels was sitting outside on the porch with her head turned in a daze.

"Hey you! You looking for somebody? Jewels? Why you out here? Jew! Just wanted some fresh air?" I asked her.

Jewels turned around and her face was bruised, not bad but, noticeable to me. She was in tears.

"What in the hell happened to your face?" I questioned her.

"Marcus and I had a fight. He said I told Trina about the situation with the punk. Trying to embarrass him." She was sobbing.

"Omg no! Jewels today I saw Trina at the doctor. She was mouthing off about you leaving Marcus alone. I can't lie friend, I told her don't nobody want her gay ass husband. I'm so sorry this

127

happened. I didn't think this would happen." I apologized.

"Doctor's office?" Jewels asked.

"Yeah Jewels, I'm pregnant." I said pulling my papers from my purse.

"Oh my God! I'm so happy for you friend, congratulations!" Jewels hugged me.

Jewels was so selfless, standing there after just being attacked by her ex lover. She took light off her own situation and turned it onto me and my special moment.

For the past couple weeks, I've been staying by Danger's house. He feels like he needs to keep me close to him. I haven't broken the news to him about

being pregnant but, I will soon enough.
It's been cool being up under him, other
than the few times he's had a couple of
his old bitches out of their mind calling
like crazy. I don't trip at all though, he
handles them well every time. Jewels
invited Me and Danger over for dinner
later tonight, to introduce us to her new
friend Phoenix. I'm excited for her long
as he treats her right, he's straight in my
book. It's still early, so I got out of bed
and went down to the kitchen, to put
something on my stomach. I walked in on
Danger talking to his grandmother.

"Come and sit down Stori." Danger
said.

"Good Morning." I greeted and took a seat at the table.

"Good Morning, my baby." Granny responded handing me a biscuit she was buttering down.

"Granny you know I would do anything for Stori, her happiness is my happiness." Danger spoke to his grandmother while staring at me.

"Baby you are a young man, you suppose to fall in love and settle down. I know you care for Stori she's a beautiful girl with the sweetest personality. What you need some space baby, you want to put me in a nursing home Derrick?" Granny responded.

"No ma'am, I'm here to care for you."
Danger said.

"And so am I." I smiled.

"I'm glad you said that Stori." Danger
reached inside of his pocket and pulled
out a black box, he sat it directly in front
of me on the table.

"Lord, my baby is turning into a man."
His grandmother cried.

Danger opened the box, to a diamond
solitaire three carat ring, from Jarods.

"Stori, you don't have to run off and
marry me today but, I want you to know
I'm serious about us." He explained.

"I'm not perfect, so why me?" I asked.

"It wasn't your perfection I was drawn
to love, it's your imperfections that make

you one of a kind. A man should support and provide for what he values. If he doesn't it loses its value. You are worth it Stori." Danger kissed my hand.

This man knows how damaged I am, and he still wants to be here. That's what made me love him even more. Before leaving to go to Jewels, we checked to make sure his grandmother didn't need anything. On our way to Jewels, Danger asked all types of questions. The only thing I told him was that, he's going to enjoy her cooking, and she's going to have her new man over to meet. We made it and everything Jewels cooked, smells great.

"Danger are you allergic to seafood?" Jewels asked.

"No, not at all." He replied.

"Okay cool! Phoenix should be here soon then we can all eat." Jewels said.

And not five minutes later Jewels Friend Phoenix had arrived. I could feel the possibility of it in my heart but, I damn sure didn't want to believe it. Jewels is gay now! Phoenix is a woman.

Chapter 15

Jewels

The Real Jewels Carver

When Stori and Danger left for the night, Phoenix volunteered to stay around and help me clean up. I can't front, I was attracted to her. Her attitude, her calmness, although she's a female I could feel a sense of protection, whenever I'm around her. Ro James A.D.I.D.A.S was playing on my surround sound. I walked into the kitchen, where Phoenix was washing dishes. Temptation had taken over me. I kissed her, wondering if I'm being to aggressive. This is very out of character for me. She pulled back.

"Jewels, I don't want you to regret anything." She said.

"The only thing I'll regret, is if nothing happens." I kissed Phoenix again.

She kissed me back, this time my back was against the wall. I turned, and Phoenix lifted me onto the counter.

"Are you sure, this is what you want?" Phoenix asked.

"I'm positive." I whispered.

My kitty felt like she had a heartbeat of her own and was thumping at a fast pace. She raised my skirt and didn't waste anytime putting in work. Phoenix took her tongue and traced her way up to my kitty cat. With the very first lick she laid on me, I moaned. Spreading my legs wider, with one leg on the countertop, and my hand on the crown of her head. Her rhythm is smooth and controlled not rushed at all. Phoenix licked the lips of my vagina over and over. Her mouth was dangerous. I moaned again, letting her know I was really feeling it. This was a first for me, so I was nervous as hell at first. Phoenix carried me to the bedroom. As soon as my head hit the pillow, I fell into a deep sleep.

The next morning, I woke up to the smell of fresh coffee, and breakfast on my bedside table.

"Good Morning, sleepy head." Phoenix spoke from the other side of the room.

"Good Morning, Thank You for this and last night." I Grabbed my coffee and we both laughed.

"Did you get any sleep?" I asked.

"No not much, it was pleasant watching you sleep all night though." She said.

"What do you have planned for today?" I ask eating on a piece of bacon.

"Nothing much, I'm gonna head out so I can get some sleep. Phoenix said standing up to leave.

I walked her to the door and came back to finish the delicious breakfast, she prepared for me. Everything was on point, it's going to give me the energy I need for today. I have a few appointments scheduled, then my Wednesday walk and talk with Stori. I left the salon a little early to meet up with Stori. She's gonna questioned me like I'm on trial for murder but, I'm ready. When I walked up, she was drinking on a smoothie from Smoothie King and giving me a side eye look.

"Well hello, Ms.Lgbt!" She smirked.

"That's right! I needed a change. I don't trust these niggas, so I'm sexually limited and don't judge me." I shrugged my shoulders.

"Ooooh, so you think a female can't bring you a disease?" Stori asked.

"Nope, I didn't say that Stori." I responded.

"I'm just making sure you ain't turning green on me." She replied.

I told Stori how me and Phoenix met. How we've been helping each other with our growth process. I also told Stori how much I appreciate her, for looking into the group sessions for me. We made our way back around the park.

"Stori, you sure been in Danger's car every day." I said.

"Surly have been, that's my man!" She turned her neck and rolled her eyes.

Our walk and talk ended, Stori was going to meet Danger at Club 108. I had to shut down my salon, and head to see Phoenix.

Chapter 16

Stori

Save Me

After my walk and talk with Jewels, I went by Club 108 to see Danger.

"Bitch, get out of the car!" The mask man yelled.

Oh my God! What the hell is going on? He forced me into the trunk of Danger's car.

"We're not gonna hurt you, just tell us where the money is okay." He closed the trunk.

141

Money!! What money?! What the hell is going on? I was beyond scared.

I have no clue who these men are. I don't know what type of trouble Danger is in or how did I end up in a trunk behind it. The car started moving and I could hear them talking. I never heard these voices before. When the car stopped, someone sat in the backseat.

"Where she at?" He asked.

"She's in the trunk, where else would she be!" A female voice said.

"We need her to tell us where he keeps the money." The male voice said.

Oh my goodness! I know that voice anywhere, it was Hakeem's voice! What does he have going on? Where are they taking me? I'm scared out of my mind. My phone and purse were inside of the car. I couldn't dial anyone to help me, I was all on my own again. Danger would save me, if he knew where I was.

"What's in her purse?" Hakeem asked.

"Some papers, she's pregnant. I already knew that, my sister told me." The female voice said.

Sister! Taylor! The female voice is Taylor. That snake ass bitch! Jewels told me not to trust her dirty ass. Taylor teamed up with my ex and got me in the trunk of a car. These motherfuckers were in cahoots! The car stopped again.

"Why didn't Zek come?" Taylor asked.

"Cause he's a pussy, talking about we're destroying his contract. Fuck that nigga." Hakeem said angrily.

"Don't do my baby that!" Taylor said.

"You weren't saying he was your baby last night, while I was fucking you." Hakeem replied.

Taylor was the bitch from the strip club! Nasty bitch was fucking Hakeem all along. That's what I get thinking a bitch was for me, when she was after my nigga dick! The car started again. Where the hell they going now?

"Don't turn around!" Hakeem said.

"Damn the cops are behind us!" Taylor says.

"Didn't I tell you not to turn the fuck around!" Hakeem raised his voice.

Oh shit, I forgot Danger has cameras inside of his car, he must've called the cops. That's when I realize the car started speeding.

"When I say jump, jump!" Hakeem told Taylor.

"What about her?" Taylor questioned.

"That's not my baby or my bitch, jump!" He shouted. BOOM!!

Chapter 17

Danger

<u>Derrick Dangerfield</u>

BREAKING NEWS!!

"This is Kerris Mctire, reporting live with channel 9 news. We're on the scene of a high-speed chase. That has ended with the vehicle crashing, into the corner store you see here. Local officers are telling reporters, to inform the community to stay inside the suspects are still on the loose. It has also been reported that there is a female victim, who was transported to a local hospital. The victim is listed in critical, high risk condition. Medical teams are working to save the pregnant woman. Again, this is channel 9 news and I'm Kerris Mctire, Susan back to you." The broadcast ended.

I stood there looking at television monitor in disbelief. I rushed out of the club and headed towards the local police department. When I walked inside, there were cops standing around.

"May I help you?" The receptionist at the desk asked.

"Yes ma'am, my fiancée Stori Jordan was involved in a car accident, in my car. Is there any way you can tell me what hospital she's in?" I stood there almost in tears and shaking.

I couldn't imagine Stori being somewhere hurting and all alone. I had to locate her and soon!

"Your name?" She questioned glancing at the officers standing behind me talking.

"Derrick Dangerfield." I handed her my driver's license, I was becoming a little impatient.

"Mr. Dangerfield, I can't release that information, at the moment. The accident is still under investigation, would you mind answering some questions by law enforcement." The receptionist asked.

My head was spinning the woman that I love is, laying inside of a hospital pregnant somewhere. I need to find Stori and make sure doctors are doing what they need to do to save her.

"Ma'am! I'm not trying to be rude but, I'm not answering no fucking questions! My heart is somewhere hurting and you're not helping me to locate her." I said.

"Mr. Dangerfield, I'm sorry but, it's proper protocol." She recanted.

"Fuck your protocol!" I knocked over the ink pen cup and exited the percent.

She could've told me which hospital Stori was in, why are they treating me like a suspect? I would never do anything

149

to hurt Stori, I love her. Now with law enforcement not wanting to help me, I took matters into my own hands. I didn't know Jewels number but, I knew exactly where she lived. I drove straight to her house. When I made it there, I was relieved to see her car in the driveway. I got out and knocked on the door.

"Danger?" Jewels said opening the door.

"Hey Jewels, Stori was involved in a car accident, it's all over the news. I don't know which hospital she's in and I need your help finding her." I said in an urgent voice.

"Omg No! Okay let me grab my keys, I'll drive." Jewels spoke without hesitation.

"No Jewels, I'll drive." Phoenix said from behind her.

"Say, it doesn't matter who drives, can we just leave now! I placed my hand over my face and shook my head.

We started with BRGB, Phoenix was the driver and Jewels went in to see if she was there. No luck, Stori wasn't there. After that we went to OLOL, I went inside she wasn't there either. Our next hospital was OHC, Phoenix pulled into the emergency entrance and went inside. When Phoenix came out, the news she had hit me like a ton of bricks.

"She's in ICU? She can't have visitors?" I repeated what Phoenix said.

"Oh shit! They gonna let me see my friend!" Jewels said gathering her things.

"Jewels, don't even try, they're not going to allow you back there." Phoenix added.

"Phoenix, how were you able to get this info?" I asked.

"The nurse at the desk, asked what was my relationship to Stori? I told her she was my sister. I gave them my number, she assured me she would call when Stori can have visitors." Phoenix told Me and Jewels.

We went back to the car, since there was nothing we could do. I exchanged numbers with both Phoenix and Jewels. They promised to reach out, as soon as they heard something. I went home and packed a sack for me and Stori. There was no way I could go to sleep, my world felt like it was falling apart. Somebody was out to get me, and they used what I love against me. I replayed the video from my car over and over.

I wanted to know who, did this to her but, by it being dark outside, it was difficult to decipher who was in the car. The images weren't clear, and the audio was muffled. It wasn't Stori I know that, I could point out her silhouette anywhere.

The next evening Jewels called, and with good news, we could go visit Stori.

She was out of ICU and in recovery. The nurse told them that Stori is doing better but, seems a little disoriented. She explained that the head trauma Stori received from the car accident, may have her a little confused or out of place. Me, Jewels, and Phoenix met at OHC.

"Hello, we are here to see Stori Jordan." Jewels told the nurse.

"Ms. Jordan is in recovery and is only allowed two visitors at a time." The nurse informed.

Phoenix stayed behind, and the nurse buzzed us through the double doors. She walked Me and Jewels to Stori's room. We walked in, Stori just laid there with monitors all over her body. Her head was

154

wrapped and turned towards the window.
I stood back and talked with the nurse,
Jewels rushed to Stori's bed.

"Hey Stori, I'm so happy to see you!"
Jewels cried.

"Hey Jewels." Stori said softly.

I sighed in relief. She looked at me
and back at Jewels.

"Hi Beautiful, I'm so happy to see
you." I grabbed her hand, as I kneeled
down beside the hospital bed.

She looked at Jewels than back at me
again, pulling her hand away from me.

"Who are you?" Stori asked.

Part Two

Coming in 2019

Also

The *Jewels Carver* Story

TANGLED *HEART*

Food Talk (southern recipes)